The Ugly Duckling

First published in 2005 by
Franklin Watts
96 Leonard Street
London
EC2A 4XD

Franklin Watts Australia
Level 17/207 Kent Street
Sydney
NSW 2000

Text © Maggie Moore 2005
Illustration © Kay Widdowson 2005

A CIP catalogue record for this book is available
from the British Library.

ISBN 0 7496 6154 2 (hbk)
ISBN 0 7496 6166 6 (pbk)

Series Editor: Jackie Hamley
Series Advisor: Dr Barrie Wade
Series Designer: Peter Scoulding

Printed in China

The Ugly Duckling

Retold by Maggie Moore

Illustrated by Kay Widdowson

FRANKLIN WATTS
LONDON·SYDNEY

Once upon a time,
there was a sad and
lonely duckling.

He was the ugliest
duckling on the pond.

He was big. The other
ducklings were small.

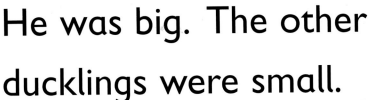

He was grey. The other
ducklings were brown.

"What a strange-looking duckling," laughed the other farm animals.

"Go away, ugly duckling!"
they cried. They chased
him far away.

The ugly duckling hid in
a reed bank by a river.

He hid in the reeds all
through the summer ...

... and all through
the autumn.

One day, the ugly duckling
saw beautiful, large, white
birds flying in the sky.

"I wish I could be like them," he thought. "Then I would fly away."

But he didn't fly away.
He hid in the reeds all
through the cold winter,
always by himself.

In spring, the ugly duckling
swam through the reeds
into the river.

Three beautiful, large,
white birds came
flying towards him.

He tried to hide so that
they wouldn't laugh at him.

But it was too late.

They had seen him.

"Why are you all by
yourself?" they asked.

"I was hiding because I'm
so ugly," he replied.

"But you're not ugly.
You're as beautiful as we
are. Look!" they cried.

He looked at himself in the river and saw, not an ugly duckling, but a beautiful, white swan.

"I'm a swan!" he whispered.
"I'm not an ugly duckling
any more!"

"Why don't you come
and join us?" said the
beautiful swans.

Then four beautiful swans
rose up into the air and
flew away together.

31

Leapfrog has been specially designed to fit the requirements of the National Literacy Strategy. It offers real books for beginning readers by top authors and illustrators.

There are 31 Leapfrog stories to choose from:

The Bossy Cockerel
ISBN 0 7496 3828 1

Bill's Baggy Trousers
ISBN 0 7496 3829 X

Mr Spotty's Potty
ISBN 0 7496 3831 1

Little Joe's Big Race
ISBN 0 7496 3832 X

The Little Star
ISBN 0 7496 3833 8

The Cheeky Monkey
ISBN 0 7496 3830 3

Selfish Sophie
ISBN 0 7496 4385 4

Recycled!
ISBN 0 7496 4388 9

Felix on the Move
ISBN 0 7496 4387 0

Pippa and Poppa
ISBN 0 7496 4386 2

Jack's Party
ISBN 0 7496 4389 7

The Best Snowman
ISBN 0 7496 4390 0

Eight Enormous Elephants
ISBN 0 7496 4634 9

Mary and the Fairy
ISBN 0 7496 4633 0

The Crying Princess
ISBN 0 7496 4632 2

Jasper and Jess
ISBN 0 7496 4081 2

The Lazy Scarecrow
ISBN 0 7496 4082 0

The Naughty Puppy
ISBN 0 7496 4383 8

Freddie's Fears
ISBN 0 7496 4382 X

Cinderella
ISBN 0 7496 4228 9

The Three Little Pigs
ISBN 0 7496 4227 0

Jack and the Beanstalk
ISBN 0 7496 4229 7

The Three Billy Goats Gruff
ISBN 0 7496 4226 2

Goldilocks and the Three Bears
ISBN 0 7496 4225 4

Little Red Riding Hood
ISBN 0 7496 4224 6

Rapunzel
ISBN 0 7496 6147 X*
ISBN 0 7496 6159 3

Snow White
ISBN 0 7496 6149 6*
ISBN 0 7496 6161 5

The Emperor's New Clothes
ISBN 0 7496 6151 8*
ISBN 0 7496 6163 1

The Pied Piper of Hamelin
ISBN 0 7496 6152 6*
ISBN 0 7496 6164 X

Hansel and Gretel
ISBN 0 7496 6150 X*
ISBN 0 7496 6162 3

The Sleeping Beauty
ISBN 0 7496 6148 8*
ISBN 0 7496 6160 7

Rumpelstiltskin
ISBN 0 7496 6153 4*
ISBN 0 7496 6165 8

The Ugly Duckling
ISBN 0 7496 6154 2*
ISBN 0 7496 6166 6

Puss in Boots
ISBN 0 7496 6155 0*
ISBN 0 7496 6167 4

The Frog Prince
ISBN 0 7496 6156 9*
ISBN 0 7496 6168 2

The Princess and the Pea
ISBN 0 7496 6157 7*
ISBN 0 7496 6169 0

Dick Whittington
ISBN 0 7496 6158 5*
ISBN 0 7496 6170 4

* hardback

3 8002 01428 0145

MEG CABOT

The
Princess Diaries

Retold by Anne Collins

MACMILLAN

ELEMENTARY LEVEL

Founding Editor: John Milne

The Macmillan Readers provide a choice of enjoyable reading materials for learners of English. The series is published at six levels – Starter, Beginner, Elementary, Pre-intermediate, Intermediate and Upper.

Level control
Information, structure and vocabulary are controlled to suit the students' ability at each level.

The number of words at each level:

Starter	about 300 basic words
Beginner	about 600 basic words
Elementary	about 1100 basic words
Pre-intermediate	about 1400 basic words
Intermediate	about 1600 basic words
Upper	about 2200 basic words

Vocabulary
Some difficult words and phrases in this book are important for understanding the story. Some of these words are explained in the story and some are shown in the pictures. From Pre-intermediate level upwards, words are marked with a number like this: ...³. These words are explained in the Glossary at the end of the book.

Answer Keys
Answer keys for the *Exercises* and *Points for Understanding* sections can be found at www.macmillanenglish.com

Contents

Notes About the Author and This Story   4
A Picture Dictionary   5
The People in This Story   6

1 I Am Mia   8
2 "You're a Princess!"   14
3 Lilly's Place   18
4 The Thermopolis-Renaldo Agreement   22
5 Grandmere   27
6 Blond Hair and Fake Nails   32
7 A New Friend   36
8 In the News   42
9 I'm Famous!   47
10 My First Date   52
11 The Wrong Kind of Boy   58
   Points for Understanding   62
   Exercises   64

Notes About the Author and This Story

Meg Cabot (Meggin Patricia Cabot) was born in Bloomington, Indiana, U.S.A. She lives in New York City with her husband, Benjamin, and her cat, Henrietta. Meg Cabot studied Art at Indiana University. Then she became an illustrator of books and magazines.

Meg's first novel, *Where Roses Grow Wild*, was published in 1988. She wrote this book using the name Patricia Cabot. Her favorite authors are Jane Austen, Judy Blume, and Barbara Cartland. Her favorite food is pizza.

Some of Meg Cabot's stories are: *The Princess Diaries* (2000), *The Princess Diaries: Take Two* (2000), *The Princess Diaries: Third Time Lucky* (2001), *The Princess Diaires: Mia Goes Forth* (2002), *The Princess Diaries: Give Me Five* (2003). The first two stories about Princess Mia were made into the movie, *The Princess Diaries* (Buena Vista/Walt Disney Pictures, 2001).

ecology the study of life on Earth and the way that people, animals and plants live together.

e-mail a way of sending messages from one computer to another. E-mail messages can be sent on the Internet to **chatrooms**. You can have a conversation in an Internet chatroom because the computer messages are instant.

environment the air, water and land on Earth, and all the living things in it.

Greenpeace an international organization which works to protect the environment.

online use a computer to talk to people on a computer network, and to search for information on the Internet.

whales the largest animals that live in the sea. There are few whales because they have been hunted and killed by people for many hundreds of years.

A Picture Dictionary

newsreporter's van

limousine

whale

penguin

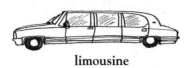
tray

$$ax^2 + bx + c = 0$$
algebra formula

olive oil

olives

pancakes

Thai Café

food carton

flashbulb

camera

high-heeled shoes

fake nails

nailpolish

pizza

sneakers

roses

boot laces

cellphone

vase

The People in This Story

Grandmere (Clarisse Marie Renaldo)

Principal Gupta

Philippe Renaldo

Helen Thermopolis

Frank Gianini

Mia (Amelia) Thermopolis
Fat Louie

Tina Hakim Baba

Josh Richter

Lana Weinberger

Doctor Moscovitz

Doctor Moscovitz

Michael Moscovitz

Lilly Moscovitz

Boris Pelkowski

Carol Fernandez

Lars

Wahim

1

I Am Mia

My name is Mia Thermopolis. I'm fourteen years old and I live in New York City. I live in an apartment in Greenwich Village, on the west side of the city. I live with my mom, Helen, and my cat, Fat Louie. My mom is an artist. She paints pictures.

I'm a freshman—a ninth grade student at Albert Einstein High School. My best friend is Lilly Moscovitz. Lilly isn't pretty but she's very smart. She is interested in politics and ecology. Lilly writes reports about the people of New York and their problems. Then she makes films of her reports. She has her own TV show—*Lilly Tells It Like It Is*. Lilly's mom and dad are doctors—they're both psychoanalysts. Psychoanalysts find out about people's feelings. Lilly has an older brother named Michael.

My parents never got married. They stopped loving each other before I was born. Fourteen and a half years ago, they broke up their relationship. My parents' relationship ended, but they're still friends.

My dad doesn't live in New York. He lives in a small country called Genovia. It's near the border of France and Italy. My dad is an important person in the government of Genovia. I visit my dad every Christmas and summer. I stay with him and Grandmere—my grandmother—in her house in France.

I'm not very popular at school. I don't have lots of friends. And I don't have a boyfriend. No boy has ever asked me out on a date because I look strange. I look like a freak. I'm the tallest girl in my grade. I have huge feet and very curly, light brown hair. I'm also very thin.

   I want to look like Lana Weinberger. Lana Weinberger is in my grade and she's beautiful. She has long blond hair and big gray eyes. Lana is going out with Josh Richter. She's dating the best-looking boy in the school. Josh is really GORGEOUS! He has blond hair and blue eyes. He's six feet tall and very good at sports. He's a senior student.

   My mom gave me this diary. She told me to write down my feelings. I don't tell her my real feelings. That's what she says. So she wants me to write them down.

Tuesday, September 23rd
My mom's right. I don't tell her about my real feelings. I

think about my feelings. But I don't tell anyone about them. I've decided to write my feelings here in my diary.

MY MOM IS GOING OUT ON A DATE WITH MY ALGEBRA TEACHER, MR FRANK GIANINI!

"I'm happy about this," I told Mom. But I'm not happy. There are about two million guys in Manhattan. She could go out with any of them. Why does she want to go out with my school's Algebra teacher?

Wednesday, September 24th

I told Lilly about my mom and Mr Gianini.

"Mr Gianini is OK," said Lilly. "He's nice and his classes are easy."

Lilly's good at Algebra. She doesn't have to work hard in Algebra classes. But I'm flunking Algebra—I fail every Algebra test. Every afternoon, after school finishes, I have to do extra Algebra.

That's how Mr Gianini met my mom. He asked her to come to the school. "Mia is flunking Algebra," he told her. "She needs to do extra work."

Then he asked my mom out on a date.

"I don't understand you, Mia," said Lilly. "Why are you hiding your real feelings? Talk to your mom. You're not happy about her and Mr Gianini. Tell her this."

But I can't talk to my mom. She's very happy about her date with Mr Gianini. She's being really nice to me. Last night, she made a special meal for me—pasta with lots of vegetables. I'm a vegetarian, so I don't eat meat.

I think about my mom kissing Mr Gianini. Then I think about Lana Weinberger and Josh Richter. I saw them kissing last week.

I want Josh Richter to kiss me like that.

Thursday, September 25th

Today, Mr Gianini asked me a really easy question, but I didn't hear it. I just sat there, looking at him.

"What?" I said.

Then Lana Weinberger leaned over my desk and stared at me. Her long blond hair touched my desk. "FREAK," she said.

I went to Lilly's apartment after school. Her parents—the Doctors Moscovitz—were there.

"Your mother is dating your Algebra teacher," Lilly's mother said. "How do you feel about that?"

"I feel fine, Doctor Moscovitz," I said. But I was lying.

Lilly's older brother, Michael, was also in the apartment. He's a senior student, like Josh Richter. But Michael doesn't play sports like Josh. Michael is only interested in computers. He spends a lot of time in his room, working on his computer. He writes an online magazine called *Crackhead*.

"Your mom is dating Frank Gianini?" said Michael. And he laughed.

11

Friday, September 26th

This afternoon, during my Algebra class, Mr Gianini spoke to me quietly. He started talking about his date with Mom.

"Mia, I'm going out with your mother," he said. "Are you unhappy about that?"

"Oh, no, Mr Gianini, it's OK," I said. I felt my face becoming red. "It's only for one date, isn't it?"

"Well, maybe I'll take her on more than one date. I really like your mother."

"OK," I said. "But if you make her unhappy, I'll kill you." I've been very rude to a teacher! Did I *really* say that to him?

Mr Gianini smiled. "Mia, I'm not going to hurt your mother," he said. "I will never upset her."

That evening, when my mom was out with Mr Gianini, my dad called from Genovia. He wanted to talk to Mom. He sounded very weird. His voice was really strange.

I didn't want to tell him about Mom and her date with Mr Gianini. I lied. "She's working in her art studio," I said.

Saturday, September 27th

I went into the kitchen early this morning. My cat, Fat Louie, wanted some food. My mom was there, and she was making pancakes! I couldn't believe it. Mom never cooks breakfast. She usually wakes up later than me. She was in a very good mood. She was smiling happily.

"I had a wonderful time last night," she said.

Mom and Mr Gianini ate dinner at a Thai restaurant last night. They're going on another date this week. I feel OK about this. I'm happy because my mom is happy.

Sunday, September 28th

My dad called again today. This time, Mom *was* in her art studio. My dad sounded very weird again.

Monday, September 29th

Today, Mr Gianini was in a very good mood. Suddenly he started talking about the school play. All the students are going to act and sing in the musical, *My Fair Lady*.

"Mia, you could play the main character," he said.

I was surprised. Mr Gianini was only being nice. I knew that. But I can't be in a musical. I can't sing—my voice is horrible.

Later, when I was with Lilly, Lana Weinberger came up to us. She started calling me a freak again. Josh Richter was with her. I knew why Lana said this. She wanted to hurt me. And she wanted Josh to see my unhappiness.

"Leave us alone, Weinberger!" said Lilly angrily.

Lana started to argue with Lilly. But Lilly isn't afraid of Lana. She just laughs if people say bad things to her.

Tuesday, September 30th

Something weird has happened. When I got home from school, my mom was waiting for me. She had a strange look on her face. She spoke softly and quietly.

"Your dad called," she said. "He's very upset. He's heard some bad news. He's sterile. He can't have any more kids."

About a year ago, my dad was very ill. He had cancer. He had an operation—doctors had to cut the cancer out of his body. Then he had chemotherapy treatment. The chemotherapy worked well and the cancer hasn't come back.

"The chemotherapy has made your dad sterile," Mom said. "He can never have another child."

I don't understand why my dad is upset. Why does he want more kids? He already has me. I only see Dad at Christmas and in the summer, but that's OK. He looks after Genovia and he's always very busy.

13

My dad's hair fell out after the chemotherapy, but he's still handsome. He looks like Captain Jean-Luc Picard in the TV show, *Star Trek: The Next Generation*. My dad has had a lot of girlfriends. He brings them to Grandmere's house in France. They love the twenty-seven bedrooms, the ballroom, the swimming pools, and the farm. But Dad never goes out with any girl for more than a few months.

"Dad is flying here, to New York, tomorrow," said Mom. "He wants to talk to you, Mia."

2

"You're a Princess!"

Wednesday, October 1st
My dad has arrived in New York. He's staying at the Plaza Hotel, where all the rich people stay.

Thursday, October 2nd. Afternoon. The Ladies' Room at the Plaza Hotel
I've had a terrible shock. Now I know why my dad wants more kids. IT'S BECAUSE HE'S A PRINCE!

My dad is a politician and he's rich. But he's also the Prince of Genovia, and *nobody* told me! I've been to Genovia lots of times. Every summer, I stay in my grandmother's house, Miragnac. It's on the border of France, near Genovia. Why didn't *she* tell me the truth?

A few years ago, I found some information about Genovia in an encyclopedia. I read these facts. The name of the Genovian royal family was Renaldo. The head of the family was Prince Artur Christoff Philippe Gerard Grimaldi Renaldo. There was a picture of the prince. He had thick brown hair and a moustache. My dad's family name is also Renaldo. My dad's name is Philippe Renaldo.

This afternoon, my dad and I sat in the Palm Court dining room at the Plaza Hotel. Lots of tourists go there. They like to have tea there in the afternoons.

"I want you to know the truth, Mia," began my dad in a very serious voice. "I am the Prince of Genovia."

This news was a terrible shock for me. Suddenly, I got hiccups!

"Really, Dad?" I said. *Hiccup.* I tried to stop the noise coming from my throat. But I couldn't. *Hiccup. Hiccup!* They were really loud hiccups! *Hiccup! Hiccup!*

"I'm head of the royal family of Genovia," said my dad. "Your mother didn't want you to know this. She didn't want you to grow up in a palace. I agreed with her. But unfortunately, I've now heard some bad news. I can't have any more children. You're my only child, Mia. So you are now my heir. When I die, you will be the ruler of Genovia."

I hiccupped again. This was really embarrassing! The people who were sitting on the table beside us were staring at me.

"Mia?" said my dad. "Are you listening?"

"Dad, please excuse me for a minute," I said. "I have to go to the bathroom."

I went into the ladies' room. The ladies' room at the Plaza is very beautiful. The walls and the carpets are pink. There are mirrors and little couches everywhere. I thought about what my dad had said. *He's the Prince of Genovia.*

I'm beginning to understand some things that I didn't understand before. When I fly to France, there's always a huge limousine waiting for me at the airport. When I go shopping with my grandmother, we always visit stores in the evening. We go shopping after ordinary people have gone home. We're always the only customers in the stores.

Most people have never heard of Genovia. Nobody famous has come from there. But it is a very beautiful country. The weather is warm and sunny. In the north, there are mountains covered with snow. In the south, there is the blue Mediterranean Sea. In the center of the country, there are hills covered with olive trees. Olive oil is Genovia's main export. Genovia sells a lot of olive oil to other countries.

There's a royal palace in Genovia. I've passed it lots of times when I was in the car with Grandmere. But she never told me who lived in it.

My hiccups have gone now. I'll go back to my dad.

Late afternoon. The Penguin House at Central Park Zoo
I've had a second shock. I'm not going to tell anybody about my family. I'm not even going to tell Lilly. She won't understand. No one will understand. I'm really upset.

This is what happened. When my hiccups disappeared, I returned to the Palm Court dining room. My dad was speaking on his cellphone. He was talking to my mom.

"Yes, I told her," he was saying. "No, she doesn't seem upset." He looked at me. "Are you upset?"

"No," I said. I wasn't upset—not *then*.

My dad ended the call. "Did you understand what I told you, Mia?" he asked.

"Yes," I said. "You're the Prince of Genovia."

"Yes," he said. "But you're not Mia Thermopolis any more."

"I'm not?" I said. "Then who am I?"

"You're Amelia Mignonette Grimaldi Thermopolis Renaldo, Princess of Genovia," said my dad, a little sadly.

WHAT? A PRINCESS? ME? It can't be true. My mouth opened but no words came out. I started to cry. My dad leaned across the table and touched my hand.

"It won't be so bad," he said. "You'll like living at the palace in Genovia with me. You can visit New York. You can see your friends as often as you want."

Then I got mad. I was so angry that I stopped crying.

"I DON'T want to live in Genovia," I said in a loud voice.

Everyone in the dining room turned and looked at me.

My dad was shocked. "Mia," he said, "I thought that you understood."

"I understand only one thing," I said. "You lied to me all my life. You never told me the truth about your family. And why do I have to live with you in Genovia?"

I stood up quickly and ran out of the hotel. I ran all the way down the street and into the middle of Central Park. It was getting dark, but I didn't think about this.

Suddenly I saw the gates of the Central Park Zoo. I've always loved that zoo.

I paid my entrance money and went into the Penguin House. The funny little black and white birds swam around their pool and I watched them. Then I sat down and took my diary out of my bag. I'm writing in my diary now. What am I going to do? I *can't* leave New York and live in Genovia.

Evening
Of course, I couldn't hide in the Penguin House for ever. When the zoo closed, I took a bus home. My mom and dad were sitting at the kitchen table. The phone was in front of them. They both began talking at the same time.

"Are you OK? Where have you been?" asked my mom.

"We've been so worried!" said my dad.

"I ran away. I'm sorry," I said.

Then I went into the bathroom and took a bath. After lying in the hot water for a long time, I put on my favorite pajamas. Then I picked up Fat Louie and went to bed. Before I fell asleep, I heard my mom and dad talking in the kitchen.

3

Lilly's Place

Friday, October 3rd. Home
When I woke up today, I felt better. It's Friday—the day before the weekend. Friday is my favorite day of the week.

Mom was in the kitchen, making breakfast. Dad was there too. He was sitting at the table and reading the *New York Times*.

And then I remembered. I'm a princess! Suddenly, I felt unhappy again.

"We need to talk, Mia," said my dad. He folded his newspaper and laid it on the table.

"Come and sit down, Mia. Have some breakfast," said my mom. "I've made everything that you like."

I didn't want to talk about my future in Genovia. "I have to go to school," I said.

"SIT DOWN!" said Dad loudly.

I sat down, and Mom put some food onto my plate.

"Mia," she said, "Think of the lovely things that you can have in Genovia. When you're sixteen, you can have a car. Dad will buy you a car for your sixteenth birthday."

"I don't want a car," I said.

"You've always wanted a horse, haven't you?" she said. "You could have a horse in Genovia. A nice gray one. . ."

My eyes filled with tears and I started to cry.

"Mom," I said, "Why are you saying this? Don't you love me any more? Why are you making me leave? Why do I have to live with Dad? Is it because you and Mr Gianini don't—"

Then my mom started crying too. She jumped up from her chair and put her arms around me.

"No, Mia," she said. "I just want the best thing for you."

"So do I," said my dad.

"Well, I want to stay here and finish high school," I said. "That's the best thing for me. Then I'm going to join Greenpeace. I'm going to save whales from danger."

"You're *not* going to look after whales!" said my dad.

"Please, Philippe," said my mom. "We can't talk about this now. Mia has to go to school. She's late."

I started looking for my coat. "Yes," I said. "I have to get to the subway station."

"No," said my dad. "Lars will drive you to school."

"But I have to meet Lilly," I said. "I meet her every day, and we go to school together on the subway."

"Lars can pick up your friend too," said Dad.

Lars is my dad's driver. He goes everywhere with my dad. But now I realize something. Lars isn't just my dad's driver. Lars is also my dad's bodyguard. His job is to protect my dad. Lars came up to the apartment and walked downstairs to the car with me. It was really embarrassing.

Algebra class

Lilly was very surprised to see Lars.

"My dad's in town and Lars is my dad's driver," I said.

"Why are your eyes red?" asked Lilly. "Have you been crying? What's happened?"

"Nothing has happened," I said. I didn't want to tell Lilly the truth.

Now I'm sitting here in the Algebra class. But I feel better. Nobody can *make* me be a princess. This is America. People are free in America. They can live in any place and in any way that they want. If I don't want to be a princess, I don't have to be one. I'll tell my dad tonight.

Late evening. Lilly's bedroom

I didn't go to my extra Algebra class with Mr Gianini this afternoon. When school finished, I spoke to Lilly.

"Can I stay at your place tonight?" I asked.

She said yes, so I called my mom.

"Can I stay the night at Lilly's apartment?" I asked her.

"But, Mia, your father wanted to have another talk with you this evening."

"I'll be home tomorrow, Mom," I said quickly. "And I won't forget to do the shopping on the way home."

Saturday, October 4th. Early morning. Lilly's place

I always have a great time when I stay with Lilly. The Moscovitzes are nice and their apartment is huge.

Lilly's parents—the Doctors Moscovitz—never forget to pay bills. They always have delicious food in their refrigerator. They even buy vegetarian food for me to eat. I love my mom very much. But she spends a lot of time in her art studio. She doesn't spend much time at home with me. Sometimes, Mom forgets to pay the bills. Sometimes, she even forgets to buy food. I want my mom to be like Lilly's mom. I want my dad to be like Lilly's dad.

At Lilly's place, I can relax. I feel very comfortable and happy there. When I'm with the Moscovitzes, I don't worry about Algebra. I don't worry about being a princess.

Last night, Lilly's parents went out. So Lilly and I climbed into their huge bed and watched James Bond movies on their big TV. Then Lilly's brother, Michael, came into the room.

21

"Your dad is on the phone," he said to me.

"I don't want to speak to him." I replied.

"OK," said Michael. "You and Lilly already went to bed. I'll tell him that."

Michael went and spoke to my dad again. Then he came back and watched James Bond movies with us. We had a really good conversation about our favorite actors and actresses. When Lilly's parents came home, Lilly and I went back to her room.

"Mia, who do you prefer?" asked Lilly. "Josh Richter, or my brother, Michael?"

"Josh Richter," I said.

I'm in love with Josh Richter. He's the best-looking boy in the school. I love his blond hair and blue eyes.

But later, I thought about Michael. He isn't as good-looking as Josh, but he makes me laugh. One time, I saw Michael coming out of his bedroom. He wasn't wearing a shirt, and he looked really good. I've never told Lilly my thoughts about her brother. She'll think that I'm weird.

4

The Thermopolis-Renaldo Agreement

Saturday, October 4th. Afternoon

I stayed at Lilly's place as long as I could today. But I was worried about my mom and dad. I didn't go home last night. Were they angry all night? I came home after lunch.

I've always been a good daughter. I don't smoke cigarettes, and I don't take drugs. I do my homework most of the time, and people trust me. I'm an honest person.

When I got home, my mom was reading a magazine. She

always goes to her art studio on Saturdays. But today she had stayed at home, waiting for me. My dad was there too. He was reading the *New York Times*.

"We must talk," he said.

"Please, Dad," I said. "I need time to think about things."

"I know," said my dad.

Then my mom came over and put her arms around me.

"We're so sorry, Mia," she said.

I was very surprised. Why were my parents being so nice? Why weren't they angry with me?

"This is difficult for you, Mia," said my dad. "We understand that now. So we've done something to make things easier."

My dad pulled a document from his pocket and put it on the table in front of me. I started to read it.

THE THERMOPOLIS-RENALDO AGREEMENT

I, Artur Christoff Philippe Gerard Grimaldi Renaldo, make this agreement. My daughter and heir, Amelia Mignonette Grimaldi Thermopolis Renaldo, can stay at her school, Albert Einstein High School. But she must spend every Christmas and every summer in Genovia.

I felt very happy. Then I read the rest of the agreement.

I, Amelia Mignonette Grimaldi Thermopolis Renaldo, will do my duties as heir to Artur Christoff Philippe Gerard Grimaldi Renaldo, Prince of Genovia. I will become the ruler of Genovia when he dies. I will also go to all the functions of state.

"What are functions of state?" I asked.

"Special ceremonies," said my dad. "When an important event happens in the world, every country sends someone— a representative. For example, when the leader of a country marries or dies, a representative of the Genovian royal family goes to the ceremony. You're the Princess of Genovia, so you will go to these functions of state. You will represent Genovia."

"But I don't know how to behave like a princess," I said.

"That's OK," said my dad. "Grandmere will teach you."

I thought about this. How can Grandmere teach me? She's not here in New York, she's in France. I signed my name at the bottom of the agreement.

Evening

It's Saturday night, and I don't have a date with a boy. I'm spending the evening with my DAD! I'm always at home on Saturday nights. Boys don't want to go out with me.

My mom has gone out on a date with Mr Gianini. She was wearing a small black dress and high-heeled shoes. My dad stared and stared at her. She looked really beautiful. Usually, my mom isn't very interested in clothes.

I phoned a restaurant that delivers food to the apartment. I ordered a pizza and some salad. It was a delicious meal. But my dad wasn't interested in the food. He watched sports programs on TV and drank whisky. Then he fell asleep.

I tried to call Lilly, but her phone was busy. Maybe Michael was chatting online with a friend.

Michael uses his computer at lot. He works on his magazine, *Crackhead*, and chats online with his friends for hours. He uses his computer to send instant messages. He has conversations in Internet chatrooms.

I really wanted to speak to Lilly. I wasn't going to tell her about being a princess. But sometimes just talking to Lilly makes me feel better.

I watched my dad sleeping. I started to get bored. I decided to send Michael an instant message. I wanted him to go offline. Then I could call Lilly.

Michael and I use different names when we chat to each other online. I'm "FtLouie," which means Fat Louie. It's the name of my cat. Michael uses the name "CracKing"—a criminal who sells drugs. Michael is clever and funny. He's always making jokes. This was our conversation:

CracKing: What do you want, Thermopolis?

FtLouie: I want to talk to Lilly. I want to speak to her on the phone. Please go offline.

CracKing: What do you want to talk to her about?

FtLouie: I'm not telling you. It's private.

CracKing: Why are you at home? Didn't Dreamboy call you? Didn't he ask you out?

FtLouie: Who's Dreamboy?

CracKing: Josh Richter, of course.

I love Josh Richter, and now Michael knows this! Lilly told her brother my secrets! I'm really embarrassed! I'm going to kill her!

But five minutes later, my phone rang. It was Lilly.

"You wanted to talk to me," she said. "Michael told me."

Michael can be so nice sometimes.

Sunday, October 5th

I didn't go to Mr Gianini's Algebra class on Friday, and he told my mom. I can't believe it! I had to stay at home today. I had to study Algebra with my DAD! There's an Algebra test at school tomorrow. I must *not* flunk it. I've written an important Algebra formula on the bottom of my sneaker. I can look at the formula during the test.

Monday, October 6th, 3:00 a.m.

I've been awake all night. I've been worrying about the Algebra formula that's on my shoe. What will happen if someone sees it? If I look at the formula, I'll be cheating. I'll no longer be an honest person. I'll have to leave Albert Einstein High School if someone finds out about this. And I'll never get a job at Greenpeace.

4:00 a.m.
I tried to wash the formula off my sneaker, but it won't come off! I can't wear my boots instead of my sneakers. The laces of my boots are broken.

7:00 a.m.
Someone will see me cheating in the Algebra test. I just know it.

$$ax^2 + bx + c = 0$$

9:00 a.m.
I'm in the girls' room at school. Lana Weinberger came in and she saw me washing the bottom of my sneaker. Then she started brushing her long blond hair, and staring at herself in the mirror. I couldn't wash the formula off my sneaker. But I'm not going to look at it during the test.

Evening
OK—I looked at the formula during the test. But it didn't help me at all. I got all the answers wrong anyway. I can't even cheat well!

I have so many things to worry about. I must buy new laces for my boots. I'm flunking Algebra. My mom's dating my Algebra teacher. I'm the Princess of Genovia. I hate my life.

5

Grandmere

Wednesday, October 8th

Grandmere's HERE! She's not here in our apartment. But she's here in New York. She's staying at the Plaza Hotel, with my dad.

Maybe Grandmere won't come to our apartment. She hates cats and Fat Louie is here. Also, Grandmere will hate Greenwich Village. No one is allowed to smoke cigarettes in the restaurants here and she smokes all the time.

Why did she have to come here? Why? Why? WHY?

Thursday, October 9th

I found out why Grandmere has come to New York. She's going to give me PRINCESS CLASSES! This is terrible. I can't write any more.

Friday, October 10th

Yesterday, after school, I had my first princess class.

It's not a joke. Every day, after my Algebra lesson with Mr Gianini, I have princess classes at the Plaza with my grandmother. I signed the Thermopolis-Renaldo Agreement. My dad reminded me about this. The princess classes are part of my duties as my dad's heir. That's what I agreed to. I checked the agreement. But I couldn't see anything in it about princess classes.

Grandmere is staying in the penthouse suite of the Plaza. She's staying in the huge, luxury rooms on the top floor of the hotel. Everything in the penthouse is colored pink. There are pink walls, pink carpets, pink drapes, and pink furniture. There are lots of vases of pink roses too.

Grandmere's name is Clarisse Marie Renaldo. She is my father's mother. She is the Dowager Princess of Genovia. Grandmere wears lots of makeup and smokes cigarettes all the time. All her clothes are purple. Purple is her favorite color. Grandmere started asking me questions immediately. She is *scary*. She frightens me.

"Stand up straight, Amelia," she said. "Your hair is too curly. And why are you so tall? Can't you stop growing? Come and kiss your grandmere."

I walked over and kissed her.

Then I saw Rommel—my grandmother's dog. He was looking out from behind her skirt. He's fifteen years old and he was wearing a purple jacket. It's the same color as Grandmere's dress.

"Now," said Grandmere, "You are Princess of Genovia. You cried when your father told you the news. Why?"

Suddenly I felt very tired. I sat down on one of the pink chairs. "Oh, Grandma," I said in English. "I don't want to be a princess. I just want to be me—Mia."

"Don't call me Grandma," said Grandmere. "I'm your grandmere. Speak French when you speak to me. Sit up straight in that chair. And your name isn't Mia—it's Amelia." She sat down in the chair next to me. "Don't you want to be a princess?"

"Grandma—I mean, Grandmere," I said, "I can never be like a princess."

"You are your father's heir," said Grandmere in a very serious voice. "When your father dies, you'll rule Genovia."

I stared at Grandmere and she stared at me. "I have a lot of homework today," I said. "Is this princess class going to take a long time?"

"We'll begin classes tomorrow," she said. "You'll come here in the afternoons, after school. Write a list before you come here tomorrow. Make a list of the ten women who you admire most. And give reasons. Bring the list with you."

My mouth fell open with shock. *Homework?* I've got to do *homework* for these princess classes?

"Close your mouth, Amelia," said Grandmere. "Tomorrow you'll do your hair nicely. You'll wear lipstick and paint your nails with nailpolish. And you won't wear those big, ugly boots. Now I have a dinner appointment. Goodbye."

Today, I borrowed one of my mom's lipsticks and took it to school. But I didn't want anyone to see me wearing lipstick. I waited until after my class with Mr Gianini. When all the other kids had gone home, I went into the girls' room. I put lipstick on my lips and brushed my hair. My hair is very curly. I brushed it and brushed it, but it didn't look better.

I'd forgotten about the school Computer Club. The Computer Club has a meeting at Albert Einstein High School every Friday afternoon. Lilly's brother, Michael, is in the Computer Club.

When I walked out of the girls' room, I met Michael. I dropped my bag and the lipstick fell out. Michael picked it up. He stared at me in surprise.

"Why are you wearing this?" he asked, holding the lipstick toward me.

"Please don't tell Lilly," I said.

"Don't tell Lilly what?" he said. "Where are you going? Are you going on a date?"

"No, I am not going on a date!" I said. "I have to meet my grandmother."

"Do you usually wear lipstick when you meet your grandmother?"

I looked toward the door. Dad's bodyguard, Lars, was standing there. He was waiting for me. He was going to drive me to the Plaza Hotel.

"Michael, don't tell Lilly about this. OK?" I said. Then I ran away.

When I got to the Plaza, Grandmere was HORRIBLE.

"You're wearing too much lipstick," she said. "And it's the wrong color for you."

I gave her my list of the ten women who I admire. But she tore up the piece of paper. "They're not good choices," she said. Then she told me to come back at ten o'clock the next morning.

"Grandmere, tomorrow is Saturday," I said. "I always help my friend, Lilly, on Saturdays. We film her TV show."

But Grandmere didn't listen to me. So when I got home, I called Lilly. I wanted to say, "I can't help you tomorrow. I have to spend the day with my grandmother." But no one answered the phone. The Moscovitz family were out.

Saturday, October 11th, 9:30 a.m.

I called Lilly early this morning. This was our conversation.

"You have to spend the day with your *grandmother?*" she said angrily. "I don't believe you, Mia. Why didn't you say 'no' to your grandmother? We always spend Saturdays together."

"Lilly, you don't know my grandmother," I said. "She's scary. I can't just say 'no' to her."

"I don't know your grandmother," said Lilly. "That's true, Mia. I don't know anything about her. It's very strange. You know all about *my* grandparents."

I've never introduced Lilly to Grandmere because Grandmere hates children. Also, she hates hearing about poor peoples' problems. Lilly makes TV films about the problems of poor people. I can't introduce Lilly to Grandmere now. I'm a princess. I don't want Lilly to know about my future life in Genovia.

"Well, come to my place tonight," Lilly said. "I have to finish my film. You can help me." Then she hung up the phone.

Now I'm in the car with Lars. We've just arrived at the Plaza Hotel. I'm going to meet Grandmere.

31

6

Blond Hair and Fake Nails

Saturday, October 11th. Late afternoon

I can never go to school again. I can never go *anywhere* again. I'm so embarrassed. I look *awful*. I'm really angry with Grandmere.

This morning, she was waiting for me in the entrance of the Plaza Hotel.

"*On y va,*" she said, which in English means, "Let's go."

"Let's go where?" I asked.

"Chez Paolo," said Grandmere. Chez Paolo means "Paul's house."

"Maybe Grandmere has a friend called Paul," I thought. "And maybe we're going to his house."

But Chez Paolo wasn't a house. It was a beauty salon, and Paolo was a stylist. He makes ordinary people like me look beautiful. That is Paolo's job. First, he cut my hair short. Then, he colored it blond. My real fingernails are very ugly because I bite them. So he stuck beautiful long fingernails made of plastic on top of my own nails. Then he put makeup on my face.

When Paolo had finished, I looked in a mirror. I got a shock. He had turned me into a different person!

Then Grandmere took me to some very expensive shoe shops and clothes shops. She bought me four pairs of shoes, and lots of clothes. Grandmere's very happy because I don't look like Mia Thermopolis any more. Mia Thermopolis never had blond hair or fake fingernails. Mia Thermopolis never wore makeup, or beautiful, expensive shoes and clothes.

But I'm not happy at all. Who am I now? I don't know. I'm not Mia Thermopolis. Grandmere is turning me into someone else. As soon as I got home, I tried to talk to my dad. But he didn't listen to me.

"What's the problem, Mia?" he said. "You look beautiful. I like your new hairstyle. It's very. . .nice."

My mom came out of her bedroom. She was wearing a new skirt and top, and she looked great. She was going out on another date with Mr Gianini. My dad stared at her.

"Mia," said my mom, "your grandmother is just trying to prepare you."

"Prepare me for what?" I said. "I'm the Princess of Genovia but I don't want anyone to know this."

"They'll find out about you soon," said my mom. "Maybe they'll read your story in the newspaper."

"Why will it be in the newspaper?" I asked.

My mom and dad looked at each other. Then my dad took out his wallet. He opened it and took out some money.

"All right, Mia," he said. "How much do you want?"

I was shocked. So was my mom.

"I'm serious," he said. "The Thermopolis-Renaldo Agreement isn't working. I want your grandmother to turn you into a princess. So I'll pay you to go to the princess lessons. How much do you want, Mia?"

I started to speak. I didn't want any money. But my dad said, "Listen. I'll give one hundred dollars a day to Greenpeace. The money will arrive with a letter from you. The money will help Greenpeace to save a lot of whales. But, you'll learn how to be a princess. Do you agree?"

I want to work for Greenpeace when I leave school. If I pay them all that money, they'll have to give me a job!

So I agreed. I'll learn to be a princess.

Evening

Lilly Moscovitz and I had a fight—a *big* argument. She isn't my friend any more! This is what happened.

I couldn't help Lilly with her film this morning. I had to go out with Grandmere. So Lilly told me to help her this evening. When I walked into the Moscovitzes' apartment, she stared at my hair.

"What *happened* to you?" she said in a shocked voice.

"My grandmother took me to a guy called Paolo. He—"

But Lilly wouldn't let me finish my explanation.

"Your hair is the same color as Lana Weinberger's," she said. "And what are those things on your fingers? Are those *fake fingernails*? Lana Weinberger has those too! You're turning into Lana Weinberger!"

I started to get angry. I am *not* turning into Lana Weinberger.

"This wasn't my idea," I said. "It was my grandmother's decision. I had to agree."

"Why didn't you say 'no' to your grandmother?" said Lilly. "I asked you to help me. But you said 'no.' Then your grandmother told someone to cut off your hair. She told them to color it yellow. And you let her do this."

I got really mad. It had been a very difficult day.

"Lilly!" I said angrily. "*Shut up!*"

I've never told Lilly to shut up before. Why was Lilly telling me what to do? Then Michael came out of his bedroom. When he saw me, he looked very surprised.

"*What* did you just say to me?" said Lilly. She was angry now.

"My mom, my dad, my grandmother and my teachers are always telling me what to do," I said. "You're my friend. Now you're telling me what to do too."

"What is your *problem*?" said Lilly.

"I don't have a problem," I said. "But you seem to have a big problem with me. So I'm leaving. And," I said, opening the door, "my hair is *not* yellow."

I went home and took a hot bath. Then I picked up Fat Louie and got into bed. Lilly hasn't called and apologized. I'm not going to call her first.

I looked in the mirror a few minutes ago. My hair doesn't look so bad.

11:59 p.m.
Lilly still hasn't called.

Sunday, October 12th. Morning
Something has just happened. It was very embarrassing.

I walked into the kitchen to get some breakfast. My mom and Mr Gianini were sitting at the table. They were eating pancakes. They were *very* surprised to see me.

"What are you doing here, Mia?" asked Mom. "You were going to stay at Lilly's place last night."

I didn't reply. At that moment, I wanted to be at Lilly's place. I didn't want to see Mr Gianini having breakfast in our kitchen. He had spent the night at our place with my mom. I didn't want to know this.

"Frank missed his train home last night," said my mom. "So I asked him to spend the night here. He slept on the couch in the living room."

She was lying—I knew that. But I didn't say anything.

Late morning

After breakfast, my mom and Mr Gianini went to Central Park. They asked me to go with them. But I didn't go. I have lots of homework to do. That's what I told them. Maybe they'll kiss each other. I didn't want to see that. People kiss on TV and that's OK. But my mom kissing my Algebra teacher? No!

Afternoon

I've just turned on my computer. I've got an e-mail from Michael Moscovitz. He's going to help me with my extra Algebra. I can't believe it! Wasn't that nice of Michael?

7

A New Friend

Sunday, October 12th. Late evening

My dad called me after lunch.

"I want you to come to the Plaza Hotel this evening. I want you to have dinner with me and Grandmere," he said. "I'll send Lars to pick you up in the car."

When I told Mom, she looked happy.

"That's OK," she said. "I'll stay here. I'll order some food from my favorite Thai restaurant. I'll watch TV."

Dinner at the Plaza was very boring. I couldn't eat most of the food because it was meat. But I ate some fish, and some chocolate ice cream.

Dad kept asking me questions about Mom and Mr Gianini.

"Do you feel OK about your mom dating your Algebra teacher?" he asked.

Why is my dad asking me this? My mom likes Mr Gianini—I know that. But does she love him? I don't know. I didn't tell my dad about Mr Gianini staying the night.

When I got home, I saw two empty cartons of Thai food in the kitchen.

"Was Mr Gianini here for dinner?" I asked my mom.

"Oh, no," she said quickly. "I was very hungry, so I ordered two meals."

My mom has told me two lies today about Mr Gianini.

Lilly still hasn't called.

Monday, October 13th. Morning

This morning, I asked Lars to stop the car at Lilly's apartment building. I wanted her to ride to school with us. But she had already left her apartment.

Afternoon

I usually sit with Lilly in our school cafeteria at lunchtime. But today, a boy called Boris Pelkowski was sitting beside Lilly. He was sitting in the seat where I usually sit. Lilly likes Boris Pelkowski because he's a great musician. Boris comes from Russia and he plays the violin. He also wears his clothes in a WEIRD way.

I got a plate of salad and looked around. Most of the tables in the cafeteria were full of students.

"Who can I sit with?" I thought.

Tina Hakim Baba was sitting at one of the tables. No other students were sitting with her. Tina's parents are very rich. Her father comes from Saudi Arabia and he owns an oil company. Tina's parents are frightened of kidnappers. Mr and Mrs Hakim Baba don't want kidnappers to take Tina. Kidnappers usually want lots of money before they release a person. People have been hurt or killed by their kidnappers. Tina's parents are very careful. They send her to school in a limousine with a bodyguard. The bodyguard follows Tina everywhere. All the other students call Tina a freak.

Tina was reading a book and the bodyguard was sitting beside her. Tina had a plate of salad, just like me. But she hadn't chosen a salad because she's a vegetarian. She'd chosen it because she's a little heavy. She wants to lose weight.

I walked over to her table and put my plate down.

"Can I sit here?" I asked.

Tina looked up in surprise. She looked at me and then she looked at the bodyguard. The bodyguard nodded.

Tina laid her book on the table and smiled. She has large brown eyes and a nice smile.

"Yes," she said. "Please sit with me."

Tina and I ate our salads and talked about school. There's going to be a dance at Albert Einstein on Saturday. I asked Tina if she had a date for the dance.

"A boy from Trinity is taking me to the dance," she replied. Trinity is a school for rich boys.

I liked talking to Tina. She wasn't a freak at all. She was really nice. When she got up to get a drink, I looked at the book beside her plate. Tina was reading a romantic novel called My Name is Amanda.

Lana Weinberger walked over to the table.

"What *has* happened to your hair, Mia?" she said loudly. "It's a horrible yellow color."

Then Tina came back, holding an ice cream. She gave the ice cream to me.

"Oh, Tina," said Lana, "did you buy that ice cream for Mia? Did your daddy give you money to buy a new friend?"

Tina was very hurt by Lana's words and her eyes filled with tears. I felt very angry with Lana. Suddenly, I took the ice cream and pushed it onto Lana's sweater. Everyone in the cafeteria stopped talking. They stared at us.

"Look at what you've done!" Lana screamed.

I stood up, and picked up my plate of salad.

"Come on, Tina," I said. "Let's go somewhere quieter."

Tina picked up her salad and followed me. Her bodyguard followed too. He was laughing. Lilly Moscovitz was staring at me. Her mouth was open with shock.

Late afternoon

I'm in a lot of trouble. I'm sitting in Principal Gupta's office. Principal Gupta is the head of the school. I was sent here because I pushed ice cream into Lana Weinberger's sweater. I'm worried. What's going to happen?

Evening

Principal Gupta has punished me. She has given me a week's detention. Every day next week, I have to stay for an hour after school, and do extra work. I also have to do my extra Algebra every day with Mr Gianini, *and* the princess classes with Grandmere.

"Lana's sweater has to be cleaned and you must pay," said Principal Gupta. "And you must apologize to her."

"I'm sorry, Principal Gupta," I said, "I'll pay for Lana's sweater to be cleaned. But I won't apologize to her."

Principal Gupta was surprised, but she wasn't angry with me.

"Mia," she said quietly, "I'm worried. You've never been in trouble before. Is. . .is everything all right? Do you have any problems at home?"

I thought about all my problems.

My mom is dating my Algebra

teacher. My best friend hates me. I'm fourteen and I've never had a date. I'm too tall and too thin. And I'm the Princess of Genovia. But I didn't want to talk about these things with Principal Gupta.

"Everything's fine," I lied.

"You're a very special person," said Principal Gupta. "You're good and kind. Lana Weinberger is just like you. She's a very nice girl too."

Principal Gupta doesn't understand. Lana Weinberger isn't like me at all!

Tuesday, October 14th

When Lars and I arrived at school this morning, Tina Hakim Baba was arriving at the same time. We smiled at each other, and went into school together. Her bodyguard followed us.

"I told my parents what happened yesterday," said Tina. "I told them what Lana said. I told them about your fight with Lana. They've invited you to dinner on Friday. You can stay the night at my house."

"OK," I said. I smiled. "Thanks."

I like Tina. She's *nice* to me.

Afternoon

I've just heard some news and I can't believe it. Lilly is going to the dance on Saturday. She's going with Boris Pelkowski! I'm the only girl in my class who doesn't have a date for the dance. THE ONLY ONE. Why am I such a freak?

8

In the News

Tuesday, October 14th. Evening
This afternoon, while Michael Moscovitz was helping me with my Algebra, he asked me a strange question.

"Are you doing anything on Saturday evening?"

A teacher came into the room before I could reply. But I knew what Michael was going to ask me. He wanted me to meet him on Saturday. He was going to help me. He was going to give me some extra Algebra work. I don't want to do extra Algebra—not on the weekend.

Grandmere is very happy. She heard about my friendship with Tina Hakim Baba. Tina's father is a rich Saudi Arabian prince. He knows lots of other rich people.

Wednesday, October 15th
When I got to school today, lots of kids were staring at me. Maybe there was something wrong with my hair. I went into the girls' room to look in the mirror. Some girls saw me. They ran out of the room, laughing.

Late morning
A *weird* thing just happened to me. Josh Richter, the most popular boy in the school, came up to me.

"Hi, Mia. How are you?" he asked.

I couldn't answer. Josh Richter *never* speaks to me. Then he bent down until his

face was close to my face. His eyes are very blue.

"See you later," he said softly. Then he walked away.

Principal Gupta's office

Now I know why everyone was staring at me. I know why the girls ran out of the girls' room. I know why they laughed at me. I know why Josh Richter spoke to me. My story is in the news!

My picture is on the cover of a newspaper—the *New York Post*. The picture shows me leaving the Plaza Hotel on Sunday night. Over the photo are the words: PRINCESS AMELIA. Underneath the picture are the words: NEW YORK'S ROYAL PRINCESS.

Mr Gianini saw the picture on his way to work. He called my mom, but she didn't hear the phone. So he called my dad at the Plaza Hotel. My dad told him to bring me to Principal Gupta's office. While I waited for my dad, I looked at the *New York Post* on Principal Gupta's desk.

I read the story about me. It was by a reporter called Carol Fernandez. She wrote about my mom and dad too. She called my mom, "the black-haired artist, Helen Thermopolis." She called my dad, "the handsome prince, Philippe of Genovia." And she called me, "the tall and beautiful princess of Genovia." Carol Fernandez must be crazy. I'm not beautiful!

"Mia, you're a princess," said Principal Gupta. "Why didn't you tell me?"

"I didn't want anyone to know," I said.

Here comes my dad now.

Afternoon

I'm mad with my dad. He made me stay at school and go back to my classes.

"You don't understand, Dad," I said. "All the kids are laughing at me. Why did you tell Carol Fernandez about me?"

"*Me?*" said my dad in a surprised voice. "I didn't tell that reporter anything." Then he looked Mr Gianini.

Mr Gianini was standing by the door. His hands were in his pockets.

"It wasn't *me*," replied Mr Gianini. "I didn't speak to Carol Fernandez. I hadn't heard of Genovia until this morning."

"Well, *somebody* told the newspapers about Mia," said my dad. "I'm going to call Carol Fernandez and ask her."

Then he told Lars to go with me to my classroom.

"Dad, I don't need a bodyguard," I said.

"Mia," said my dad. "Genovia is a small country but it's very rich. Maybe someone will try to kidnap you."

"Dad, no one is going to kidnap me," I said.

But my dad didn't listen. Now I have a bodyguard, just like Tina Hakim Baba. Everyone will laugh at me even more.

Late afternoon

Suddenly I'm very popular. When I walked into the cafeteria at lunchtime, Lana Weinberger came up to me.

"Hey, Amelia," she said. "Come and sit with us!"

Lana wants to be my friend now, because I'm a princess.

"No, thanks, Lana," I said. "I have someone to sit with."

I went to sit with Tina. Lana looked shocked. Everyone in the cafeteria was staring at our table. Tina looked at me sadly, but she didn't say anything.

"Tina," I said at last. "If you don't want to sit with me, I'll understand."

Tina's eyes filled with tears. "What do you mean, Mia?" she said. "Don't you like me any more?"

"Of course I like you," I said. "But everyone is staring at us because of me."

"No, Mia," she said. "They're not staring because of you. Everyone always stares at me. They stare at me because of Wahim."

Wahim is Tina's bodyguard. He and Lars were sitting together at our table. The two men were talking about guns.

I got mad then. I wasn't mad with Tina. I was mad with everyone else at Albert Einstein High School. Nobody talks to Tina. "She's a freak," they say. "She's weird." But she's a really nice girl.

"I want to sit with you, Tina," I said.

Tina looked happier then. She started reading another

romance today. She told me all about it.

When Michael Moscovitz was helping me with my Algebra, we had this conversation. Lilly joined in too.

MICHAEL: So you're the Princess of Genovia? When were you going to tell your friends?

ME: I didn't want anyone to know.

MICHAEL: Why? It's not a bad thing.

ME: Are you joking? Of course it's bad. I don't want a different life. I don't want to be a princess.

LILLY: Mia, your dad has more than three hundred million dollars. He's never worked for it. I read this in a newspaper. Did this money come from the poor people of Genovia?

MICHAEL: Lilly, no one in Genovia has to pay anything to their government. The country is very rich. Everyone in Genovia has a good education. Maybe Mia's father gets paid well because he works very hard for his country. You're jealous.

LILLY: I am *not*!

MICHAEL: Yes, you are. Mia got a new hairstyle, and she didn't ask for your advice first. That's why you're jealous. Then you stopped talking to her, and she found a new friend. All this time, Mia had a secret. And she didn't tell you about it.

LILLY (to Michael): Michael, *shut up*!

MICHAEL (to me): Does this guy (pointing to Lars) follow you everywhere? Does he go with you on dates? Will he go with you to the dance this weekend?

ME: No, because no one has asked me.

9

I'm Famous!

Wednesday, October 15th. Evening

I'm famous. When Lars and I walked out of the school today, there were reporters everywhere. They started taking photos and shouting questions.

"Smile, please, Amelia!"

"Hey, Amelia, what's it like being a princess?"

I was frightened but Lars helped me. First, he told me not to say anything. Then he put his arm around me. He pushed me through the crowd of photographers and reporters. He pushed me into the back seat of Dad's car. Then he jumped in beside me.

"Drive!" shouted Lars.

I didn't know the man who was driving the car. My dad was sitting next to him.

"Where will I go to school now, Dad?" I asked.

"You can stay at Albert Einstein High School," said my dad. "Lars will go with you every day. He'll protect you."

"Who will drive your car?" I asked.

"Hans," said my dad, pointing to the driver. "He's my driver now."

"Will Lars go everywhere with me?" I asked.

"Yes," said my dad.

Suddenly, I understood. I'll never be able to go anywhere alone again.

"I don't want to be a princess any more," I said. "You can take back your money. Tell Grandmere to go back to France. I've had enough."

"It's too late, Mia," said my dad. "You are the Princess of Genovia. Everyone knows that. Tomorrow, there will be photos of you in every newspaper in America."

Later

My mom spoke to my dad. Now he's mad with her.

"Clarisse talked to Carol Fernandez about Mia, didn't she?" said Mom.

"My mother didn't tell that reporter about Mia," said my dad angrily. "Why do you think that? Maybe your boyfriend, Frank Gianini, spoke to the reporter."

Then my mom got mad too. "Get out," she said in a cold voice. "Leave my apartment."

"You don't like my mother, so you can't see the truth," said my dad angrily.

"The truth?" said my mom. "I'll tell you the truth, Philippe. Your mother. . ."

I went to my room. I didn't want to hear the fight between my parents. But is my mom right? Did Grandmere tell Carol Fernandez about me?

Thursday, October 16th

This morning, my picture was on the covers of the *Daily News* newspaper, and the magazine, *New York Newsday*. The picture was also in the *New York Times*.

There were more reporters waiting for me outside school today. Lars held my arm and we ran into school together. As we ran, the reporters were shouting questions.

"Amelia, who do you like best—Leonardo DiCaprio or Prince William?"

"Princess Amelia, why don't you eat meat?"

Afternoon

Something very surprising has happened. I was in the cafeteria with Tina and Lars and Wahim. We were eating our lunch.

Suddenly, Lana Weinberger put her tray down next to mine. I'm not joking—Lana Weinberger sat beside me. Then someone else put down a tray on the table. It was *Josh Richter*.

"Hey," he said. He sat down in the seat next to me, and started eating.

"Are you going to the school dance this weekend, Mia?" asked Lana. "Josh's parents are away. After the dance, we're all going to a party at Josh's place. Will you come too?"

"I'm sorry," I said. "I can't."

Lana stared at me. "What do you mean, you *can't*?" she said.

I've heard about the seniors' parties. Everyone drinks lots of alcohol and gets very drunk.

"My mom won't let me go to a party like that," I said.

"Don't tell your mom the truth," Lana said. "Say to her, 'I'm spending the night with a girlfriend.'"

But I could never tell this lie to my mom.

"I'm sorry," I said, "Everyone drinks a lot of alcohol at those parties. I don't drink alcohol. Alcohol is a poison. I don't like putting poison into my body."

"I can understand that," said Josh Richter suddenly.

"Josh!" said Lana, laughing. "You drink more than anyone in the whole school."

Josh didn't laugh. He just stared at Lana with his blue eyes. It wasn't a very nice stare.

Late afternoon

When classes finished, Josh was waiting outside my classroom.

"Hey," he said. Then he smiled. It was a big smile that showed all his teeth. They were very white.

"Are you going to the dance with anyone?" he asked.

I dropped my book in surprise. I bent down to pick it up. "N–no," I said in a weak voice.

"Oh. Well, I'll see you," said Josh. Then he left.

I'm still shocked. Josh Richter talked to me today. *Twice*.

Evening

This evening, Grandmere wanted to have dinner at an expensive restaurant. She wanted us to go outside the Plaza Hotel for a meal.

"There will be reporters outside," she said. "I'll teach you what to do." But when we came out of the hotel, the reporters weren't there.

"Wait one minute," said Grandmere. She went back into the hotel. I got into the car. She came out of the hotel again a little later.

When we arrived at the restaurant, lots of reporters were waiting. I was very surprised. Immediately, they started taking photos and shouting questions.

I turned to Grandmere. "You called these reporters, didn't you? You told them about our plan to eat here. Did you tell Carol Fernandez about me too? Did you give her my story for her newspaper?"

"Of course," said Grandmere. "You have to learn how to live with reporters, Amelia. It's part of being a princess."

"Dad and Mom had a big fight about the report in the *New York Post*," I said. "But Mr Gianini didn't talk to Carol Fernandez, did he? You did. I'm going to tell Dad the truth. He's going to be really mad at you, Grandmere."

"No, he won't be mad," she said. "That story in the *Post* was only the beginning. Soon you'll be on the cover of *Vogue* magazine, and then—"

"Grandmere!" I shouted. "I DON'T WANT TO BE ON THE COVER OF *VOGUE*!"

When I got home, I called my dad. "Dad, Grandmere told Carol Fernandez everything about me," I said. "It wasn't Mr Gianini."

"I know," he said in an unhappy voice.

"Well," I said, "you have to apologize to Mom."

Later, my dad called my mom. Afterwards she looked very happy. Maybe my dad apologized to her.

10

My First Date

Friday, October 17th

JOSH AND LANA HAVE BROKEN UP! I can't believe this. Josh has ended his relationship with Lana. He doesn't want her as his girlfriend any more. Everyone in school is talking about it.

When I saw Lana, she looked awful. Her eyes were red— she had been crying.

After the first lesson

Josh Richter came up to me after my English class.

"Hey, Mia, who are you going with to the dance tomorrow?" he asked.

"Er. . .no one," I replied.

"Well, why don't we go together?" he said.

I couldn't speak for a minute. JOSH RICHTER AND ME ON A DATE!!!

Then I heard a tiny voice inside my head. *He's only asking you because you're the Princess of Genovia.* But I didn't want to listen to the voice.

"Yeah, OK," I said. "That might be fun."

"Fine," said Josh. "I'll come for you at seven o'clock. We'll go to a restaurant—Tavern on the Green—and have dinner first."

Late morning

I'm going to the dance with Josh, and Lilly has found out. Now she's speaking to me again. But she only says bad things about Josh.

"He's just broken up with Lana," she said. "He broke up with her *sixteen hours ago*. Then *this afternoon* he asks you out. He's bad, Mia. And he takes drugs."

Some of Josh's friends take drugs—this is true. But does Josh take drugs? I can't believe that.

Lana looks so sad, and Josh doesn't seem to care. He and his friends sat with Tina and me at lunch today. But Josh and his friends didn't talk to us. They just talked to each other. I feel bad about Lana. But I still want to go to the dance with Josh.

Evening

My princess class with Grandmere ended after an hour. This is because I'm going to spend the night at Tina's place.

I told Grandmere about the dance and Josh's invitation. Grandmere was very pleased. She called a famous fashion company. She made an appointment for me tomorrow. I'm going to their store to choose a new dress.

After I left Grandmere's suite, I went to Tina's huge, luxury apartment. Tina has three little sisters and a baby brother. She also has a big TV in her room, and a Sony Playstation.

Tina's parents are really nice. Mr Hakim Baba isn't well. He has a problem with his heart. He can't eat meat. He only eats vegetables and rice. Mrs Hakim Baba is very beautiful. She's British and she has blond hair. She used to be a fashion model. Her picture was once on the cover of *Vogue*, but she doesn't work now.

Tina showed me her dress for the dance. It's very pretty. She looks much more like a princess than I do.

Saturday, October 18th

When I got home, Mr Gianini was there.

"Has Josh called?" I asked my mom.

"You don't mean Josh Richter, do you?" asked Mr Gianini.

"Yes," I said. "I'm going to the dance with Josh tonight."

"But what about Lana Weinberger?" asked Mr Gianini in a surprised voice. "She is Josh's girlfriend."

"They broke up,' I said.

"Who's Josh Richter?' asked my mom.

"He's the most gorgeous boy in the school," I said.

"Well, he's the most popular," said Mr Gianini. "But he isn't the right kind of boy for Mia."

"Oh," said my mom. "Then I have to talk to Mia's father."

She called my dad at the Plaza Hotel. As she was speaking to him, the front door bell rang. Mr Gianini opened the door.

"I'm Clarisse Marie Renaldo—the Dowager Princess of Genovia," said a loud voice. "Who are *you?*"

It was Grandmere! She had come to our apartment. She was going to take me shopping. She stared at Mr Gianini.

"Grandmere," I said, "they won't let me go to the dance."

My mom was still talking to my dad on the phone. Grandmere came into the apartment and took the phone from Mom's hand.

"Philippe," Grandmere said into the phone. "Your daughter is going to the dance tonight with her boyfriend. I'm going to buy her a new dress. I'm taking her to the store now."

Then Grandmere spoke quickly to my dad. She used some rude words. But she spoke in French, so only I understood her. My mom and Mr Gianini didn't understand what she was saying.

When Grandmere put the phone down, she looked around our apartment. "The Princess of Genovia lives *here*?" she asked. "In *this* place?"

"Now listen, Clarisse—" said my mom angrily.

"Go and get your coat, Amelia," said Grandmere.

I went to get my coat. When I returned to the living room, my mom's eyes were very red. Mr Gianini was looking at the floor. Then I went shopping with Grandmere. Mom and Mr Gianini didn't stop me.

Evening

It's after seven o'clock and I'm waiting for Josh. I'm sitting and writing my diary.

I'm wearing my new dress and my new shoes. My hair and my makeup and nails are perfect. My dress is pale blue silk and it's beautiful.

My dad is sitting at the kitchen table. My mom keeps looking at the clock.

"You can go out with Josh," said my dad, "but Lars has to go with you."

My dad looked at his watch. "It's seven-fifteen," he said. "Josh Richter is late."

The front door bell has just rung. Josh is here!

The Ladies' Room, Tavern on the Green

I'm sitting in the Ladies' Room of the restaurant—Tavern on the Green.

Josh was good with my parents. My dad asked him lots of questions. Questions such as: What car are you driving? What time will you be back? Which college are you going to after high school?

Josh answered all my dad's questions politely. He even called my dad "Sir"!

Then Josh and Lars and I went down to the street. Josh had come in his father's car. We got into it. Lars drove, and Josh and I sat in the back seat. We talked for a few minutes, but then a strange thing happened. Josh and I didn't have anything more to say to each other. We didn't talk for the rest of the ride to the restaurant. I don't have this problem with Lilly's brother Michael. Michael Moscovitz and I never stop talking.

When we got to the restaurant, Josh's friends and their girlfriends were sitting at a big table. Josh ordered bottles of champagne. Then, without asking me, he ordered steaks too. But I'm a vegetarian and I won't eat meat.

I haven't eaten my steak and Josh hasn't noticed. He's talking and laughing with his friends. He hasn't spoken to me since we got to the restaurant. He has ordered more and more champagne. Why does he want to drink so much?

This evening is not going well, so I came into the Ladies' Room. But I'll have to go back to the table soon.

11

The Wrong Kind of Boy

Saturday, October 18th. Evening. The Girls' Room, Albert Einstein High School

I've found out THE TRUTH about Josh. I CAN'T BELIEVE WHAT HE'S DONE!!

We stayed in the restaurant for a long time. Josh and his friends drank nine bottles of champagne. We were late getting to the dance.

When we arrived at the school, there were lots of news reporters' vans outside the building. There was a big crowd of reporters. They were shining big bright lights onto the steps at the front of the school. Some reporters were checking their cameras and tape recorders. Others were talking on their cellphones. They were all waiting for someone—me!

Who told all the reporters that I was coming to the dance? Not Grandmere this time.

Lars was very angry when he saw the crowd. But Josh didn't care. "Come on," he said to me. "We'll run up the steps into the school while Lars parks the car."

Josh held my hand and pulled me out of the car. Then he pulled me up the steps to the school doors.

When the reporters saw me, they shouted, "It's her! It's Princess Mia!"

They started taking pictures and shouting questions. The lights of the cameras' flashbulbs were very bright. I couldn't see where I was going. I held Josh's hand tightly.

At last, I saw the school doors in front of us. Josh stopped. Below us, the reporters were screaming questions and taking photos. "Kiss her! Kiss her!" they shouted.

Suddenly Josh turned toward me and kissed me on the lips.

At once, all the cameras' flashbulbs went off. The reporters were taking pictures of Princess Mia's first kiss. But I didn't feel happy and romantic. I felt embarrassed. Josh turned to the reporters. He waved his hand and smiled. Then he opened the doors to the school and pushed me inside.

My friends were standing inside the school hall—Tina and her boyfriend, Lilly and Boris. Mr Gianini, and other students from school were there too. Everyone was looking at me.

I couldn't think clearly. Josh Richter had just kissed me on the lips. He had kissed me, and all the reporters had taken a picture. Then I realized the truth. *Josh wanted to date a princess. So he broke up with Lana. Then he invited me to the dance. He told the reporters about the dance. He told them about me. He wanted to get his picture in the papers with me.*

I turned and stared at Josh. "Why did you kiss me in front of everyone?" I asked angrily.

"The reporters were shouting 'Kiss her! Kiss her!'" said Josh. "They wanted a good photo. So I kissed you."

"You didn't kiss me because you like me," I said. "You kissed me because I'm the Princess of Genovia."

"Of course I like you," said Josh.

"No," I said. "You don't care about me. You don't know me. You don't know my feelings or thoughts. You haven't asked what I like. You ordered a steak for my dinner, but you didn't ask me first."

My friends were all staring at Josh.

"Mia is a vegetarian, you idiot," said Lilly.

"Oh, sorry," said Josh. But he didn't sound very sorry. "Are you ready to dance?"

I didn't reply. I didn't want to dance with Josh. I turned and walked away into the girls' room.

Tomorrow, pictures of Josh kissing me will be in all the newspapers. Will the words: YOUNG ROYAL IS IN LOVE be above the pictures? I'm not in love with Josh any more. I don't want a boyfriend like him. He only wants me because I'm a princess. When my dad sees the photos, he's going to be really mad.

Then I heard Lilly and Tina's voices. They had come into the girls' room.

"Are you OK, Mia?" Lilly asked in a kind voice. "I'm sorry about everything. Come and join us."

"I can't," I said. "You all have dates. I don't have one."

"Michael is here," said Lilly. "He doesn't have a date."

Michael Moscovitz is at the dance? I'm coming out!

Sunday, October 19th. Lilly's place

Lilly and I aren't fighting any more. And Lilly and Tina have become friends. There weren't any pictures of Josh kissing me in the newspapers today. There was more important news. Yesterday, Iran attacked Afghanistan. All the news reports were about the fighting.

I had a wonderful time with Michael at the dance. We talked a lot, and we danced together. It was wonderful standing close to Michael and holding him.

Then we all went back to Lilly's place in Tina's car. I called my mom. She let me stay with Lilly last night.

This morning I woke up early. I can hear Lilly's family making breakfast in the kitchen. I AM SO HAPPY!

Evening. My apartment

Grandmere and Dad came here this afternoon. They wanted to know about the dance. I didn't tell Dad about my kiss with Josh. I spoke to Lars earlier. He promised not to tell my dad either!

I won't have any princess classes for a whole week. Grandmere is going away for several days.

Later in the afternoon, I took Grandmere up to the roof of our apartment. My mom and dad came out onto the roof too. There is a wonderful view of the city from our roof. You can see all of Manhattan and the Hudson River.

The sun was just going down, and the sky was purple and pink and orange. We all stood on the roof and watched the beautiful sunset. I felt very peaceful and happy. Maybe everything is going to be all right. Maybe my life as a princess will be OK too!

Points for Understanding

1

Mia tells us about her home, her family, and her friends. What does she say about herself and her wishes?

2

Mia is told two things that shock her. What happens when she hears each piece of news?

3

Mia enjoys staying at the Moscovitzes' apartment.
(a) Why?
(b) What happens when she stays this time?
(c) What does Lilly ask Mia?
(d) What does Mia think then?

4

"But I don't know how to behave like a princess," Mia says to her father.
(a) What is his answer?
(b) Why does Mia sign the Thermopolis-Renaldo Agreement?

5

Which word does Mia use to describe Clarisse Marie Renaldo? Why does she use it?

6

Why do Mia and Lilly have a fight?

7

Principal Gupta asks Mia if she has any problems.
   (a) Why is Mia having a meeting with the principal?
   (b) What is Mia worried about?

8

After Mia's Algebra class, Michael, Lilly and Mia have a conversation. Lilly says to Michael, "Shut up!" Why?

9

Why do these people get angry or upset?
   (a) Mia
   (b) Helen Thermopolis
   (c) Philippe Renaldo

10

Is Mia's date with Josh going well? Why? Why not?

11

Mia has her first kiss.
   (a) Who kisses her?
   (b) What does she feel about this?
   (c) What happens next?
   (d) What does she realize?
   (e) Who dances with her?

Exercises

Multiple Choice 1

Tick the correct answer.

Q1 Who was Philippe Augustus Grimaldi Renaldo?
a Mia's uncle
b Mia's grandfather ✓
c Mia's father

Q2   What was Philippe Augustus Grimaldi Renaldo's title?
a Prince of Ruritania
b Prince of Andorra
c Prince of Genovia

Q3   In which year did Philippe Augustus Grimaldi Renaldo marry
Clarisse Marie?
a 1960
b 1962
c 1968

Q4   What family name did Clarisse Marie take when she married
Prince Philippe?
a Grimaldi
b Renaldo
c Thermopolis

Q5   Who is the only child of Prince Philippe Augustus and Princess
Clarisse?
a Mia's uncle
b Mia's mother
c Mia's father

Q6   What happened to Arthur Christoff Philippe Gerard Grimaldi
Renaldo in 1989?
a He married Helen
b His father died
c His mother died

Q7   What is the family name of Mia's mother?
a Thermopolis
b Grimaldi
c Renaldo

Q8   Why is Mia's family name Thermopolis and not Renaldo?
a Her mother did not want to be a princess
b Her mother and father were not married
c Mia's father did not want his wife to change her name

Q9   What did Arthur Christoff Philippe Gerard Grimaldi Renaldo
become in 1989?
a Mr Thermopolis
b A father
c Prince of Genovia

Word Focus

Write the correct nationality.

COUNTRY (noun)	NATIONALITY (adjective)
Genovia	*Genovian*
Liberia	
Australia	
Algeria	
Austria	
India	
Russia	
America	
Colombia	
Italy	
Germany	

True or False?

Write T (True) or F (False).

1   Mia's mother is an actress.   ☐ F

2   Mia's father was bald because he wanted to look like a character from *Star Trek*.   ☐

3   Michael Moscovitz wrote an online magazine called *Crackhead*. ☐

4   Mia thought Michael was really boring.   ☐

5   Mia wrote an Algebra formula on her shoe so she could cheat during a test.   ☐

6   Mia's grandmother smoked all the time.   ☐

7   Lilly fell out with Mia because she was jealous that Mia was a princess.   ☐

8   Mia pushed an ice cream onto Lana Weinberger's sweater.   ☐

9   Tina Hakim Baba's parents didn't like her hanging out with Mia.   ☐

10   Mia drank too much champagne at the restaurant with Josh.   ☐

Country Profiles

Look at the list of facts about Ruritania and the Country Profile that follows it.

NAME	Ruritania
GOVERNMENT	Monarchy
HEAD OF STATE	Prince Michael (succeeded 1996)
POPULATION	123,000 (2001 census)
LOCATION	on the border of Austria and Italy
ECONOMY	largely agricultural; principal export is wine; a large source of revenue is banking services

Ruritania is a monarchy. Prince Michael became Head of State in 1996. The population of Ruritania was 123,000 (one hundred and twenty three thousand people) in 2001. The country is located on the border of Austria and Italy. Its economy is largely agricultural and its principal export is wine. In addition, a large source of revenue is banking services.

Now read the list of facts about Genovia. Write a Country Profile of Genovia using the model above.

NAME	Genovia
GOVERNMENT	Monarchy
HEAD OF STATE	Prince Philippe (succeeded 1989)
POPULATION	64,000 (1999 census)
LOCATION	on the border of France and Italy
ECONOMY	largely agricultural; principal export is olive oil; a large source of revenue is tourism

_____
_____
_____
_____
_____
_____
_____
_____

Choose the Word

I, Artur Christoff Philippe Gerard Grimaldi Renaldo, make this agreement. My daughter and heir, Amelia Mignonette Grimaldi Thermopolis Renaldo, can stay at her school, Albert Einstein High School. But she must spend every Christmas and every summer in Genovia.

I, Amelia Mignonette Grimaldi Thermopolis Renaldo, will do my duties as heir to Artur Christoff Philippe Gerard Grimaldi Renaldo, Prince of Genovia. I will become the ruler of Genovia when he dies. I will also go to all the functions of state.

Circle the correct word in each sentence.

1 This agreement is **formal** / *informal.*
2 Amelia and her father will both **sign** / **signature** this agreement.
3 Amelia's mother must also put her **sign** / **signature** on this agreement.
4 The word *heir* sounds like **hair** / **ai**r.
5 An heir is usually a close **friend** / **relative**.
6 The agreement **adds** / **changes** Renaldo to Amelia's family name.
7 Renaldo is the family name of Genovia / Genovian rulers .
8 Amelia is **allowed** / **agreed** to stay at school.
9 Amelia has to visit Genovia three times / twice a year.
10 The word *duties* is the plural of **dutie** / **duty**.
11 To do her duties means that she will **obey** / **agree** her father.
12 Prince Philippe is the **ruler** / **government** of Genovia .
13 The *functions of state* are important **events** / **shows**.
14 Another word for *go to* special occasions or *go to* school regularly is **greet** / **attend**.
15 Amelia will become the **Prince** / **Princess** of Genovia.

The Princess Classes Story

Complete the gaps. Use each word in the box once.

Genovia   school   news   tired   Amelia   classes   ~~Renaldo~~
makeup   all   cried   kissed   shorter   straight   purple   call   color
questions   list   never   mother   curly   heir   French
admire   frightens

Grandmere's name is Clarisse Marie [1] _Renaldo_ . She is my father's
[2] .... She is the Dowager Princess of
[3] ....

Grandmere wears lots of [4] .... and smokes
cigarettes [5] .... the time. All her clothes are
[6] .... Purple is her favorite [7] ....
Grandmere started asking me [8] .... immediately.
She is scary. She [9] .... me.

"Stand up [10] ...., Amelia," she said. "Your hair is
too [11] .... And why are you so tall? Can't you stop
growing? Come and kiss your Grandmere."

I bent down and [12] .... her. Grandmere is much
[13] .... than me.

"Now," said Grandmere, "You are Princess of Genovia. You
[14] .... when your father told you the
[15] .... Why?"

Suddenly I felt very [16] .... I sat down on one of the
pink chairs. "Oh, Grandma," I said in English. "I don't want to be a
princess. I just want to be me – Mia."

"Don't [17] .... me Grandma," said Grandmere. "I'm
your Grandmere. Speak [18] .... when you speak to
me. Sit up straight in that chair. And your name isn't Mia – it's
[19] ...."

"Grandma – I mean, Grandmere," I said, "I can [20]...................................
be like a princess."

"You are your father's [21]....................................," said Grandmere in a
very serious voice. "We'll begin princess [22]...
tomorrow," she continued. "You'll come here in the afternoons, after
[23].. . Write a list before you come here
tomorrow. Make a [24]... of the ten women you
[25]... most. And give reasons. Bring the list with
you."

Making Sentences

Write questions for the answers

> **Example**   *Where does Grandmere stay (in New York)?*
> ANSWER   Grandmere stays at the Plaza Hotel in New York.

Q1   *What*
A1   The name of Grandmere's dog is Rommel.

Q2   *Which*
A2   Mia attends Albert Einstein High School.

Q3   *When*
A3   She goes to see Grandmere for princess lessons after school.

Q4   *Why*
A4   Mia did not know that she is a princess because her parents never
    told her.

Q5   *Who*
A5   Mr Gianini is a teacher.

Q6   *Where*
A6   Helen Thermopolis works in a studio.

Q7   *Who*
A7   Michael and Lilly Moscovitch are Mia's friends.

Q8   *What*
A8   Doctor Moscovitch is a psychologist.

Q9 *Why*
A9 Tina Hakim Baba has a bodyguard because her father is very rich.

Q10 *Is*
A10 No, Fat Louie is not a dog – he is a cat.

Multiple Choice 2

Choose the best answer to each question.

Q1 What is Michael Moscovitz's main interest?
a Computers ✓ b Algebra c Music

Q2 What movies do Lilly and Mia like to watch?
a Love stories b Action movies c Horror films

Q3 What is the name for a person who does not eat meat?
a Vegetable b Vegetarian c Vegetation

Q4 What subject does Mr Gianini teach?
a Music b Art c Algebra

Q5 What is Ms Gupta's job at Albert Einstein High School?
a Principle b Principal c Princess

Q6 What are the films that Lilly Moscovitz makes about?
a The people of New York b School sports c Ecology

Q7 Who told the reporter Carol Fernandez that Mia was a princess?
a Mr Gianini b Mia's father c Mia's grandmother

Q8 What are Lars and Wahim?
a Bodyguards b Kidnappers c Racing drivers

Q9 Who is Lana Weinberger's boyfriend?
a Boris Pelkowski b Michael Moscovitz c Josh Richter

Q10 What is the nationality of Tina Hakim Baba's mother?
a Saudi Arabian b Iranian c British

Macmillan Education
Between Towns Road, Oxford OX4 3PP
Macmillan Publishers Limited
Companies and representatives throughout the world

ISBN 978-0-230-03747-2
ISBN 978-1-4050-8064-4 (with CD edition)

The Princess Diaries: Take One by Meg Cabot. Copyright © Meg Cabot 2000

Illustrated by Karen Donnelly
Cover illustration by Nicola Slater
Original cover template design by Jackie Hill
Additional design by Anne Sherlock

Printed in Thailand

2015 2014 2013
10   9   8   7

with CD pack
2014 2013 2012
16 15 14 13